EYE FOR AN EYE

EYE FOR AN EYE

an award-winning suspense novella by

STEPHANIE BLACK

Covenant Communications, Inc.

Cover images: *Selective Focus Half-Face Closeup Photography of Female's Green Eyes* by Jan Krnc at Pexels.com; *Person on Forest Photo* by Kiwihug at Unsplash.com.

Cover design copyright © 2021 by Covenant Communications, Inc.
Cover design by Jaren Petty, Deborah Barnard, and Kimberly Kay

Published by Covenant Communications, Inc.
American Fork, Utah

Printed in the United States of America
First Printing: May 2021

28 27 26 25 24 23 22 21   10 9 8 7 6 5 4 3 2 1

ISBN: 978-1-52441-818-2

PRAISE FOR STEPHANIE BLACK

"With a rich cast of believable and eccentric characters and a mystery to be solved, the reader can be guaranteed an entertaining read."

—Netgalley review

"Stephanie Black is a master storyteller, and she proves it with Eye for an Eye. As the mystery grows, so does the tension—right up to the wonderfully satisfying conclusion. There's no doubt readers will love this page turner."

—Sian Ann Bessey, author of *The Gem Thief* and *An Uncommon Earl*

"With fast-paced intrigue and a touch of romance, reading Eye for an Eye by Stephanie Black was like tasting a favorite treat only to find myself wanting more.

—Ronda Gibb Hinrichsen, author of *A Revolution of Hearts*

"Even in the short-story format, Black weaves a complete and exciting tale with relatable characters, an intriguing mystery, and a splash of romance. I was hooked from page one."

—Jennifer Moore, author of *Solving Sophronia* and *Inventing Vivian*

"Bound in Shallows will keep readers hooked to the pages as they piece together a tangled puzzle of blackmail and buried secrets. Stephanie Black is one of my favorite mystery authors—and books like this are the reason why."

—A. L. Sowards, author of *The Redgrave Murders* and *Of Sword and Shadow*

"Stephanie Black is a master of the unexpected. Blackmail never looked so twisty."

—Paige Edwards, author of *Deadly by Design*

"If you want to read a mystery that truly tests your deductive sleuthing abilities, Stephanie Black's Bound in Shallows, the fourth book in the Natalie Marsh series, will keep you guessing until the very end."

—Kathi Oram Peterson, author of *A Stranger Watches*

"Stephanie Black is the absolute master at keeping her readers guessing who the bad guy is to the very end. Bound in Shallows is no different. It is a classic who-done-it with heroes and heroines you love to cheer for and villains you love to hate. You simply must read this novel!

—Gregg Luke, author of *Plague* and *Deadly Undertakings*

ACKNOWLEDGMENTS

THANK YOU TO EDITOR ASHLEY Gebert of Covenant Communications and Suzy Bills, teaching professor of editing and publishing and director of the Faculty Publishing Service at Brigham Young University. I'm thrilled to have had the opportunity to participate in the Story Catchers Contest, a partnership between Covenant and the BYU editing department.

Thank you to Deborah Barnard and Jaren Petty for their stellar editing. Deborah and Jaren were a pleasure to work with, and their skill and insights helped create a richer, deeper, stronger story. They also designed this stunning cover.

For sharing their expertise, thank you to Justin Rasband, Shauna Rasband, Marshall McConkie, and Dianna Hall.

Much gratitude to Heather B. Moore, whose gracious invitation first brought this story into being. Thank you also to Annette Lyon and Heather Horrocks.

As always, thank you to managing editor Samantha Millburn, publicist Amy Parker, and all the wonderful people at Covenant.

CHAPTER 1

A CALL AT SEVEN IN the morning? Mallory Ingram switched off the vacuum she'd been threading between cubicles and pulled her vibrating phone out of her hip pocket. The display read *Michael Holmes.* Mallory paused, index finger hovering over the screen. Uncle Mike never called—though if he were to call, this would be a reasonable time for him to do it, since he never slept in past five-thirty and couldn't understand why anyone would want to.

As she swiped the screen, her tired brain realized it wasn't seven in California like it was here in New York. It was four. Heartbeat speeding up, she lifted the phone to her ear. "Hello?"

A raspy throat-clearing was Mike's only response. She waited for a few seconds, but he didn't speak. Was he sick?

"Uncle Mike?"

"Morning, Mallory," he said gruffly. "How's school?"

"Um . . . it's good. Are you okay?"

"Fine," Mike said. "Heard some bad news, though. Nelson Sanders is dead. I figured you'd want to know."

What? Mallory stared dazedly at the row of windows showing the grayish glow of a cloudy October sunrise. "What happened to him?"

"Prison riot. Heard about it on the news last night, but it was too late to call you. A couple of gangs got in a fight. Nelson got mixed up in it."

"Nelson was in a prison gang?" Two images of Nelson muddled together in her mind: the wisecracking friend sitting across from her at a table in the library while they did more chatting than studying, and the desperate drug addict she'd seen running from her house, blood staining his T-shirt.

"News report didn't say he was in a gang, just that he was one of the casualties. Lot of prisoners got hurt. Two guards killed as well." Mike paused. "You studying hard? Keeping up in all your classes?"

Only Uncle Mike would drop shattering news and follow it up with mundane questions about school. "I'm working hard," Mallory said numbly. "Grades are fine."

"Good girl. Keep at it." Mike hung up.

Mallory shoved her phone into her pocket and gripped the handle of the vacuum. Nelson was dead?

Maybe she should be happy about that. Scales of justice.

Tears filled her eyes.

Don't, Mallory. Not now. You need to finish vacuuming. You need to study for your botany midterm. You need to work on that English essay.

English essay. Nelson, plopping his scarred netbook on her lap. *"Proofread this for me, Mal-ware. Make it fast. It's due in six minutes."*

How was his family handling the news? Mallory didn't know much about his mother, except that she could punch hard enough to fracture Nelson's jaw. His older sister, Lori, had been his lifeline. Lori must be crushed by grief.

The lock buzzed from the other side of the expanse of empty cubicles. *Darien?* She'd never seen anyone else here this early. For the past few weeks, the hope of running into Darien Thomas had splashed a little fun into a dull predawn janitorial shift, but she didn't want to see him while she was crying. She'd be careful not to vacuum near his cubicle until she'd calmed down.

Oh, Nels. What had happened at the prison? She couldn't imagine him jumping into a prison fight. He'd probably been trying to stay out of the way, not wanting trouble, not wanting to hurt anyone—

Not wanting to hurt anyone.

Tears refilled her eyes. She wiped them away, took her phone, and tried to type Nelson's name and Salinas Valley State Prison into the search bar. Her fingers quivered, hitting the wrong letters.

Footsteps approached, soft thumps against the carpet. Whoever had entered was heading toward her, not toward Darien's cubicle. Not wanting to be caught Googling and weeping while she was supposed to be cleaning, Mallory tried to stuff her phone back into her pocket but missed. The phone hit the floor.

She bent to snatch the phone and stow it as the footsteps came closer. Keeping her face lowered, she knelt and picked at a staple stuck in the carpet, hoping the intruder would ignore her as he or she passed by.

The footsteps stopped. "Good morning, Mallory."

Darien. "Morning," she said. With a quick movement, she used her shoulder to wipe a tear off her cheek, then regretted it. When she'd dressed this morning, hoping to run into Darien, she'd chosen a cute lime-green cardigan she'd found at Goodwill on Saturday. *And* she was wearing makeup. Pre-Darien-crush, she never would have bothered with makeup before work. Now, she'd probably smeared mascara all over her new sweater.

"Staple in the carpet." She tried to sound casual as she pulled it loose. She rose to her feet, catching a blurry peripheral-vision view of big feet in brown leather shoes, long legs in khaki Dockers, and wide shoulders in a striped shirt. She fidgeted with the staple, aimlessly straightening it, and prayed the next installment of tears would wait until Darien had headed off to his cubicle.

"One of many staples in the carpet, I'm sure," he said. "Thanks for sparing our feet."

She dropped the staple into the wastebasket in the nearest cubicle. "So . . . you're here early again. Do you ever sleep?"

"At night I do. It's morning. The sun's even up."

"The sun beat you? How embarrassing." Her joking tone faltered. She swallowed. "You sound like my uncle."

"Mallory . . . are you okay?"

Fresh tears spilled. Why had she fooled herself into thinking she could hide how upset she was? Had she hoped he'd assume her eyes were wet and red from tears of joy she'd shed at the chance to use her favorite vacuum again?

"I'm just sleep-deprived," she said, compelling herself to meet his eyes—deep brown eyes tinted with green, a striking contrast to his platinum hair and pale skin. Simply walking across campus on a summer day must give him a sunburn. "I'm fine."

He smiled at her, but the concern in his face didn't fade.

"I'd better get back to work," Mallory said. "Have a great day." She switched on the vacuum.

CHAPTER 2

DARIEN SAT IN HIS CUBICLE, listening to the drone of the vacuum from the other side of the room. What was Mallory upset about? He couldn't ask. He hardly knew her.

He'd probably made it cringingly obvious he *wanted* to know her. Lately he'd taken to showing up at the crack of dawn—or earlier—pretending that early mornings in his grad-student cubicle were ideal for productivity. Granted, there *were* advantages to being here instead of in his apartment—no sticky spots gluing his papers to the table, no stale pizza giving off greasy odors, no roommate snoring—but until recently, he'd come in the early mornings only when deadlines had swamped him.

The urge to come here more often had kindled a few weeks ago, when he'd been here before sunrise eating breakfast while finishing a presentation for the statistics class he was teaching. He'd reached to add milk to his Tupperware container of Rice Krispies and had knocked the container to the floor, scattering cereal so widely that he'd spent a dumbfounded moment contemplating cereal dynamics before he'd crunched across the blast zone to ask the janitor if he could use the vacuum after she'd finished with it. Coming face-to-face with her for the first time had made him want to dump his cereal every morning if that would give him an excuse to talk to her.

Whenever he'd seen her after that, he'd had trouble not staring. Shiny, dark hair curving around her chin; a smile that made her whole face radiate light. He couldn't stop himself from grinning when she'd start singing along with whatever was playing through her earbuds, then stop abruptly, realizing she was soloing without accompaniment.

He'd run into her twice more before he'd had the guts to introduce himself and ask her name. Since that first meeting, he'd made sure *not* to show up unshaven and wearing a holey Bowman College sweatshirt like he had the first time he'd spoken to her.

Maybe the button-down Oxford is over the top, he thought, surveying his striped shirt. *Go for it, champ. A six-foot-five-inch beanpole math geek with more bone than muscle, but wow, you can rock that business casual. Just ask her out. If she says no, at least you can start getting over her.*

She probably already had a boyfriend. But she'd said she didn't know many people in Birch Falls yet, that she was living with her sister and brother-in-law. She was from California and hadn't started college right after high school—she'd blushed when she'd told him this was her first year at Bowman, that she was an "old granny" in freshman-filled classes. He guessed she was in her early to mid twenties.

Ever since he'd introduced himself, she would pause when passing his cubicle and switch off the vacuum to smile and ask how he was doing and what he was working on. She was a biology and secondary education major, and he'd worried the ramblings of a doctoral student in applied mathematics would bore her, but she always appeared interested and asked thoughtful questions. He'd started looking up biology facts on Wikipedia, wanting to sound intelligent when she talked about the botany class she enjoyed.

Smart, beautiful—and tall. It was nice to chat with a woman who actually came up past his shoulders. Darien always had to fight the impulse to offer to vacuum for her or take over dusting some of the countless desks and shelves. Offering to help with a job she was paid to do would trigger weirdo alerts *and* make it obvious he was into her.

Today, the urge to help her with her work wasn't the only factor making it difficult for Darien to remain in his cubicle. He wanted to offer support and find out why she was crying, but she was as far from his cubicle as she could get, vacuuming an area he knew she'd already covered—she always followed the same path when vacuuming. She'd backtracked to keep away from him.

It's none of your business. If she wanted to tell you what the problem is, she would have. She doesn't need you to fix anything.

He reached for his computer, but his thoughts remained stuck on Mallory. He pried at them with logic. *Just because she's friendly doesn't mean she wants more than a shallow friendship, talking to you at six or seven in the morning because there's no one else around. She's made it clear she doesn't want to confide in you. What are you going to do—corner her while she's wiping windows and pressure her to say what's wrong until she freaks out and avoids you forever?*

Grimly, Darien rested his fingers on the keyboard. *Focus, idiot. Focus.*

CHAPTER 3

SITTING IN HER SISTER'S KITCHEN, Mallory stared at the laptop perched on Eden's polished-oak table. Frowning, Mallory deleted a line and re-typed it. The sentence still sounded like a kid using words too big for her to handle. She backspaced again and thought wistfully of her job in Gilroy making milkshakes and mopping garlic ice cream off the tile. She'd done well in that job. But trying to access the part of her brain she'd shut down four years ago . . . No, *five* years ago; her senior year of high school had been a waste. When she'd bothered to even attend class, she'd slept through it.

For the third time, she reworded the line. She would *not* fail at Bowman. She would *not* lose her grip on the goals she'd worked so hard to dig from a mountain of inertia. Up until her mother's death, Mallory had always planned on college, had always been a good student . . .

She blinked at the screen, wishing she'd picked a different subject for her essay than writing about why life science programs should receive more focus in school curriculums. This topic kept stinging her with reminders of her mom sitting at her creaky roll-top desk, venting about budget cuts and correcting piles of fifth-grade papers.

Get to work, Mallory lectured herself, but her fingers remained limp on the keyboard. In the two weeks since Uncle Mike's call, the only thing Mallory had felt able to concentrate on was Nelson. She'd searched for news articles about the prison riot, reread articles about his arrest and trial, and even dipped into old text conversations in which she and Nelson had joked about homework and weekend plans.

Should she send his sister a sympathy card? Mallory hadn't known Lori well, but recalled she'd been an expert at getting herself and Nelson both into and out of trouble, and he'd hero-worshipped her. Mallory should definitely write to Lori. She likely hadn't received much sympathy after Nelson's death.

Will she want to hear from me? Mallory had no idea. She and Nelson's family had avoided each other after his arrest.

She scooted her chair back from the table. Tomorrow, she'd call Uncle Mike to find out if Lori still lived in Gilroy. Maybe reaching out to Lori would help her work through her own confusing grief.

She picked up her metal water bottle and refilled it with water from the fridge dispenser. On the fridge hung a dry-erase calendar filled with Eden's fastidious handwriting. She'd even added Mallory's class schedule for each day. Mallory couldn't fathom why Eden needed the calendar when she kept the same information on her phone.

After jogging around the kitchen a few times to stretch her muscles, Mallory sat at the table and reread the opening to her essay. It sounded decent, finally. She checked her outline and started on the next paragraph.

The rattle of the front doorknob stalled Mallory halfway through a new sentence. Eden and Clint were home from their early dinner with one of Clint's university colleagues. Mallory closed her laptop and gathered her books. Clint and Eden had been generous in inviting her to live in their spare bedroom, but Mallory didn't want to push her luck by being underfoot too often. She scanned the kitchen. A drop of chili marred the counter near the microwave. She snatched the dishrag and wiped it up.

Her sister and brother-in-law walked into the kitchen. Eden's dark hair was in a sleek French twist, and blond Clint looked sharp in a navy blazer and gray slacks. Clint held a paper sack.

"Hey," Mallory said. "How was dinner?"

Neither of them smiled. "Fine," Clint said, his boyish face cold. Eden stood next to him, her posture rigid.

Had Clint and Eden had an argument? Mallory couldn't decide if she should acknowledge the negative vibes or pretend she didn't notice. In the six weeks she'd been living with them, she hadn't witnessed any conflict worse than an occasional crabby word, but Clint was under immense pressure right now, worrying about his upcoming tenure decision.

"I'm going to go see if I can finish this English essay before I fall asleep on my keyboard," Mallory said. She stacked her books on her laptop and picked everything up. "Good night."

"Mal, we need to talk." Eden's voice wobbled.

Oh no. Had she done something to upset them? Mallory inventoried her recent blunders: the night before garbage collection, she'd parked at the spot on the curb where Clint always set the bins; on a beautiful day, she'd left her bedroom window cracked open when she'd gone to campus; and she'd forgotten her laundry in the washer for three days, creating a mildewy pile of clothes that had taken several additional washings to clean. But Eden had already spoken to Mallory about these issues, and Eden didn't usually harp on things that were resolved. Mallory must have done something new. "Sure, we can talk," she said lightly. "What did I do now?"

"Have a seat," Clint said.

A sit-down conversation. Mallory placed her belongings on the table and took her seat. Eden sat by her. Clint remained on his feet.

"Do you know anything about this?" Clint opened the paper bag and upended it over the table. Two plastic bags fell from the larger sack. One contained a small amount of white powder, the other a handful of white, blue, and green pills.

Thoughts of Nelson, sobbing, burst from Mallory's memory. *"I'm really sorry, Mallory. I didn't mean to hurt her. My mind was shot. When she walked in on me, I panicked."*

Mallory picked up her bottle and gulped water to ease her dry throat. "No. I don't know anything about those."

"I found these bags in my makeup drawer," Eden said. "When I was getting ready to go to dinner. I took them with me to make sure they didn't . . . disappear . . . before we could talk about them."

"Obviously, I didn't put them there," Mallory said.

Tears welled in Eden's eyes. She didn't speak.

"Eden! How can you think I'd—"

Eden brushed tears away without damaging her makeup. "I wasn't home when you were in high school, but Mom and I *did* talk."

Mallory's face burned forest-fire hot. "Okay, I was stupid. But I never did drugs."

"Really? You hung out with your druggie friends—"

"They didn't start out that way! We'd been friends since elementary school. I know I shouldn't have kept hanging out with them—"

"Mom worried about you, but she was pretty naive. You'd tell her nothing was happening at the parties you went to, and she'd believe you. I've learned from old friends of mine what really went on at those parties, and you were in the middle of it. Then you threw your own party."

Mallory fought to keep herself calm. Eden had never mentioned any of this, and Mallory had hoped she didn't know the details about that night. "Yeah, I went to parties where people were using drugs, but I didn't try them myself, and I didn't mean for my party to go that direction. I told them not to bring any of that stuff."

"Oh, give me a break. You knew they would, and you wouldn't have invited them if you weren't okay with it."

Mallory clamped her hands around the sides of her computer and stared at the textbooks on top of it as though nailing her attention to evidence of her life now would keep her from toppling into the pain and guilt of the past. Did Eden blame her—

Of course she blames you. It's your fault.

Don't think about Mom. Focus on what's happening right now and handle it.

"How long has this been going on?" Eden asked. "Years? This was part of your problem after Mom died, wasn't it?"

"No."

"I thought you were getting your life together. That's why Clint and I invited you to move in with us. But we won't put up with drugs in our house."

Mallory gestured at the baggies on the table, her hand trembling. "If those were mine, I wouldn't be dumb enough to put them in your drawer."

Clint picked up the two small bags and dropped them into the paper sack. "Unless you meant to hide them in your drawer and were too high to know what you were doing."

Mallory pictured the drawers Clint and Eden were talking about. The old bathrooms in this house had pedestal sinks and little storage space, so Eden had put an antique dressing table in a nook at the end of the hallway. The top drawer on the left held Eden's hair and makeup supplies; the one on the right held Mallory's.

"Look," Clint said. "We're not calling the police. But we're also not enabling this by giving you a cheap place to stay while you blow your money on drugs and wreck your life."

"Those are not my drugs! Who else has been here lately?"

"No one." Eden gave Mallory's water bottle a sideways glance. Was she thinking of opening it and sniffing to make sure it was water in there? "The drugs were put in my drawer sometime after I got ready for work this morning and before I got home this afternoon. No one else has been here, unless you had visitors. Did you?"

Mallory shook her head. "Someone must have broken in."

Clint loosened his tie. The cranberry stripes in the tie perfectly matched Eden's blouse; Mallory figured Eden had chosen it for him. "To *leave* drugs?" he said. "People on drugs break in to steal things, not leave them."

Nausea washed through Mallory's stomach. She inhaled deeply and wiped her sweaty hands on her jeans.

Eden's bloodless face made it plain she too was thinking of their mother's death. "Clint, we know that," she said quietly.

"I'm sorry." Clint rubbed his temples with stiff fingers. "I didn't mean to—"

"I didn't put the drugs there." Mallory held her hand out for the paper bag. "I'll take this to the police. Maybe they can lift some fingerprints."

"Clint and I both touched it," Eden said.

"There could be other prints."

Clint shook his head. "Let's not turn this into a charade. We know you have no intention of taking it to the police. You just don't want to lose your stash."

Flailing through a waterfall of anger in search of rationality, Mallory said, "Let's buy a drug test from the pharmacy. I can prove—"

"So I'm supposed to stand with my ear to the bathroom door and check to make sure you—" Eden's nose wrinkled. "We already know you're keeping drugs in our house. I'm not going to play games with you, trying to figure out if your friends taught you how to cheat a drug test."

Mallory jumped to her feet. "Clint, give me the drugs. If you don't believe I'm going to the police, come with me."

Clint furrowed his brow. She hoped her invitation had jarred him enough to get him listening instead of blaming.

"Let's go," she said.

He folded the top of the bag. "It won't work out like you think. If you show up with this bag and tell them what happened, they'll assume you're trying to preemptively cover for yourself because you're afraid we'll turn you in."

"I'm willing to try it anyway."

"You'll get charged with possession, or worse," Clint said. "You'll get thrown out of school. You might go to jail."

Mallory stomped to the entryway with Clint's crisp footsteps and Eden's clacking heels following her. She grabbed her jacket and purse from the coat closet and yanked her keys out of her purse. "Give me the bag. If you think it's mine, then give me my 'property.' I'm taking it to the police."

"You'll only make the situation worse for yourself," Clint said. "Leave the police out of it. I'll get rid of the drugs. If you'll admit you have a problem and agree to get help, we won't kick you out of the house."

Mallory wanted to leap forward and snatch the bag from Clint. Was he honestly afraid she'd make things worse for herself? She suspected he was more afraid of scandal—of the police showing up, the neighbors gossiping, and word reaching the computer science department at Bowman that Assistant Professor Clinton Westcott was involved in a drug investigation.

"Mal, please promise you'll get help," Eden said. "My doctor can recommend—"

Mallory opened the front door, marched out, and slammed it behind her, bouncing Eden's autumn-apple wreath off the hook. The sight of a man towering near the porch made her gasp.

Darien Thomas, holding a bouquet of flowers.

CHAPTER 4

"UH . . . HI." DARIEN STOOD WITH one foot on the bottom step, seemingly afraid to continue toward her. "Uh . . ."

"Hi." Mallory's dignity shriveled like the dried leaves that had blown onto the porch. She picked up the wooden wreath and hung it on the door. The red paint on one of the apples had chipped. Great. She'd better find paint to match it before Eden noticed.

"Uh . . . I . . . you've looked stressed at work the last couple of weeks, and I . . . wanted to say I hope . . . you're all right." Darien stepped tentatively onto the porch and held out the bouquet. "Didn't mean to disturb you."

Mallory took the flowers. "Thank you. Um . . . I'm sorry about . . ." The humiliation of having Darien see her like this split open another crack in her composure. She all but buried her face in the red, orange, and yellow gerbera daisies, hoping Darien wouldn't wonder why she was so eager to smell flowers that didn't have much of a scent.

"I don't want to interrupt your evening," he said. "Obviously you're on your way out. I just wanted to stop by quickly. I hope you don't mind that I looked up your address."

"I don't mind." She blinked a few times to ward off impending tears then looked up at him. "Thank you for the flowers. These are beautiful."

"You're welcome." He stepped backward off the porch, not looking where he was going, and bumped into an urn of chrysanthemums.

"Oops, sorry." He grabbed the teetering urn. "I show up and almost wreck the place."

"Finishing what I started." Mallory glanced at the damaged wreath and tears escaped. She bowed her head over the daisies again and hoped tonight's chilly autumn wind would dry her face.

"Mallory." His voice changed from embarrassed to gentle. "I don't want to hassle you, but is there anything I can do?"

She shook her head. A few more tears watered the daisies.

"Do you want me to leave?"

She didn't want him to see her bawling into a bouquet, but she didn't want to send him away either. Not when she'd been hoping he'd reach out to her outside of their early-morning conversations. Not when he'd done such a sweet thing.

She struggled for composure. If she wanted him to stay, the gracious response would be to invite him inside, but she'd rather shiver on the porch until morning than face her sister and brother-in-law with Darien as a witness.

"Can I help you put on your jacket?" he asked. "It's cold tonight."

Her jacket. She had it draped over her arm. Darien stepped forward, took the jacket, and held it open for her, a polite gesture that neither of them seemed to know how to execute. He held the coat too high, and, in an awkward attempt to find the armholes, Mallory nearly dropped the flowers. He lowered the coat, and she still fumbled to get her arms into the sleeves, this time dropping her purse. By the time she was wearing the jacket, they were both laughing.

"I need to practice that." Darien picked up her purse. The porch light showed a crimson flush in his pale face.

Mallory wiped her cheeks and took the purse. "Me too."

"Now that you're not freezing, could I take you wherever you were going?"

"I don't know where I was going. I just needed to get out of the house."

"Then . . . would you like to go somewhere with me?"

She nodded, hoping he'd have a suggestion of where. She was preoccupied trying to restrain new tears and wondering if she had any Kleenex in her purse.

"There's a chocolate shop near campus," Darien said.

Mallory smiled. Darien responded to crying by offering chocolate? He was a genius. "Yes. Let's go."

He extended a hand to help her down the stairs. Holding her purse and flowers in one hand, Mallory clutched his fingers with the other and didn't let go as he led her to his car, a Toyota pickup. The cab was spotless and smelled like Tide laundry detergent.

He drove toward campus. After a few silent minutes while Mallory stared out the window and cradled the flowers in her arms, he said, "Would you feel better if you talked about it?"

"I'm not sure. It's crazy."

"I don't mind. What is it?"

Anxiety clashed with a frantic need to confide in someone who might be an ally. Darien sounded compassionate now, but what if she told her story and he assumed she was a liar? Who else could she tell? Uncle Mike? He'd be worried about her, worried the drugs *were* hers, worried he didn't know how to help her.

"If you don't want to say anything, I won't pressure you," Darien said. "But if there's any way I can help, I'd like to do that."

"I'm actually not freaking out about the same thing that's been bothering me for a while. Well, it's related to that, but not . . . I guess it's not really related, but I'm still upset about . . . actually it *is* related, but it's a different . . ." Mallory bit her lip. "Sorry. I'm not good with the English language right now."

He chuckled. "Maybe just give the facts and don't worry about the framework yet."

Mallory surrendered to the urge to confide in him. "My sister and her husband think I'm using illegal drugs. I'm not."

"Why do they think that?"

Grateful the level of compassion in Darien's voice hadn't dropped, she related what Eden had found and what Eden and Clint had assumed. "The drugs are *not* mine. I've never used street drugs, or misused prescription drugs." Her tongue dry, she tugged a flower petal, gently so she didn't rip it loose. "My mom was killed by a drug addict."

"I'm so sorry." Darien touched her shoulder then put his hand back on the steering wheel. "How long ago did she die?"

"Five years. I was seventeen, at the end of my junior year." Mallory folded her arms around the flower stems and touched her chin to the edge of the cellophane wrapping. "When Clint and Eden showed me that stash tonight, I said I'd take the drugs to the police so they could investigate, but Clint wouldn't let me."

"Why not?"

"He said it would just make things worse for me, but I don't think that's the reason. I think he's concerned about gossip. He's a professor at Bowman, and his tenure decision is coming up. I think he's afraid involving the police would be professionally embarrassing to him. Besides, he's so sure the drugs are mine that he doesn't see the point of an investigation. I even offered to take a drug test, but Eden just made a snarky remark about me fooling the test. And I guess all a test could prove is that I haven't done drugs *lately,* but that doesn't mean I'm innocent."

"Can't you turn the drugs over to the police even if your brother-in-law doesn't want you to?" Darien asked. "He doesn't have the right to keep you from doing that."

"He won't give them to me. He and Eden have made up their minds. If I don't admit to my drug problem and get help, they'll kick me out of their house. How am I supposed to get help for a problem that doesn't exist? If they do throw me out, how am I going to afford the rent on a new place?"

Darien parked at the chocolate shop. "Do you think Clint might be trying to cover for himself? That the drugs are his?"

"He's always seemed like a trustworthy guy." Mallory ran a fingertip along the petals of a yellow daisy. "He was a jerk tonight, but it's hard to blame him if he thinks I brought drugs into his house. I can't imagine the drugs are Eden's, either. She's so in control of herself, so organized, and drugs . . . take control away."

"Besides finding the drugs, do your sister and her husband have any other reason to think you're—" Darien shut his mouth and looked away from Mallory.

Mallory focused on the brown and white awning over the entrance to the chocolate shop and silently finished the question Darien had cut off: *Do your sister and her husband have any other reason to think you're an addict?*

She couldn't stop a blush from searing her cheeks, but she wasn't offended that he'd asked—or almost asked—such a reasonable question. If she pretended she didn't know what he'd stopped himself from saying, that would flatten an honest conversation into a superficial one, and she didn't want that. But if she tried to explain, she'd start crying again.

Just keep it short.

"I made some dumb decisions in high school—hung out with people I shouldn't have. I didn't do drugs, but my mom worried about me, and she told Eden."

"So bad choices in friends from years ago? That's why Eden thinks you're guilty now?"

"It's not just that. I've had a . . . um . . . a hard time since our mom died."

Darien unzipped the top of his jacket. He was wearing a tie. Had he come from a dress-up event, or had he put the tie on for her? Even in her distress, the possibility of his dressing up for her glimmered in a warm thought: *He's adorable.*

"I can't imagine *not* having a hard time after losing your mother like that," Darien said.

"My father was long gone," Mallory added. "He left when I was six, remarried, then died of a heart attack in his late forties."

"I'm sorry."

"Eden's eleven years older than I am. She was already done with college and working in Manhattan when our mom died."

"Is that when you moved in with her?"

"No. She didn't have room. She was in a tiny studio apartment. My mom's brother Mike lived a few miles away from us. He took me in."

"Did that work out?"

"Yeah . . . sort of. He's a good guy, but his sons were already grown, and his wife was dead. He . . ." She trailed off. She didn't want to say anything critical of Mike. He'd done his best.

"He just had no idea what to do with a grieving teenage girl?" Darien suggested.

She sighed. "I fell apart. I almost didn't finish high school, but a couple of teachers dragged me through. After graduation I worked part time at an ice-cream shop and spent the rest of the time sleeping or watching TV. I just didn't care about anything. No energy."

"That's more than grief," Darien said. "That sounds like clinical depression."

"Yeah." She pulled out the envelope tucked between the flowers and the cellophane and studied her name written on it. Darien's handwriting was narrow and a little sloppy. "It took Uncle Mike and me a long time to figure that out. He finally hauled me to a doctor. When I started feeling better, I wanted to go to school, but it took me a while to get here. Eden was really supportive. She suggested applying to Bowman and offered to let me live with them my first year, but . . . Eden doesn't know me that well. She's always had trouble understanding how I could have stalled out for so long. Now she's assuming drug abuse was part of my problem. But I swear, the only drugs I took were those my doctor prescribed, and I took them exactly as she told me to . . . You didn't want to know all this history. I'm sorry for chucking my baggage at you."

"I *asked* you about this, Mallory. You don't need to be ashamed that you've struggled."

"Thank you for listening. Maybe we should get a few pieces of fudge, and you can take me home before I start crying again. It still counts as home. I have a key, and Clint hasn't had time to change the locks."

"He won't do that."

"Not tonight, at least," Mallory said.

Darien's long fingers curved around her shoulder with a kind, comforting strength. "Let's look at this situation rationally. If the drugs aren't yours and you don't think they're Clint's or Eden's, who else could have put them there?"

"Eden said no one else was in the house during the period when they could have been stashed there."

"You mean she doesn't *know* of anyone who was there. How many people have keys to the house?"

"Besides Clint, Eden, and me? I don't know. I'll ask Eden if any of her friends do." Mallory winced. "Yikes, that'll be a fun conversation."

"How long have Clint and Eden lived in that house?"

"Two years."

"Were the locks rekeyed when they moved in?"

"I don't know."

"So a former owner might have a key. Or someone could have broken in. Have Clint and Eden checked for any evidence that someone jimmied a lock or climbed in a window?"

"I'm sure they haven't. They immediately assumed the drugs were mine, so why would they?"

"Okay, that's something to investigate."

"The biggest question is *why* would someone sneak in, stash drugs, and leave?"

"No idea," Darien said. "Motive is another thing we need to establish. Let's go get that chocolate. It'll help us think."

CHAPTER 5

SEVERAL CHOCOLATE TURTLES AND TWO hours later, Darien dropped Mallory off at home and said goodnight with a quick, shy hug. She still felt mentally sore, but not as panicky. She had concrete plans—small, probably ineffective plans, but at least they were a starting point. Tomorrow, after a night's sleep had calmed Clint and Eden down, she'd ask them if anyone else had keys to the house. She'd examine windows and doors for signs of forced entry. She'd try again to convince Clint that they should take the drugs to the police—if he hadn't already flushed them. She'd check with neighbors to learn if any of them had noticed anyone approaching the house during the period when the drugs had been planted.

What if no one did approach the house? She desperately wanted to find an outside explanation for the drugs, but she couldn't ignore the fact that the most likely culprit was Clint or Eden, attempting to hide behind Mallory.

Evaluating that possibility stung like she was clutching a knife by the blade, judging the sharpness by letting it sink into her hand. There had to be a different answer. Could it have been a student angry at Clint over a failing grade, trying to stir trouble between Clint and his wife? Or a client from the bank Eden managed, angry at a rejected loan application and hoping to damage her marriage?

Bracing herself, Mallory stepped into the house. The lights in the living room and kitchen were off, but the ones in the back of the house were on.

You don't have to talk to them tonight. Go into your room and shut the door.

Mallory opened a kitchen cupboard and took out a ceramic vase. She filled it with water, unwrapped the flowers, and stuck them in the vase. The stems were too tall for the vase, but she'd trim them tomorrow. Right now, even that minor task sounded exhausting.

She opened Darien's card. No message; he'd written only *To Mallory* and signed his name. Had he been stumped as to what to write? Smiling, she tucked the card between a red daisy and an orange one.

She headed down the hallway toward her bedroom. To her surprise, *her* bedroom light glowed. Inside her room, she found Eden pulling clothes out of her dresser drawers. Clint stood in front of the open closet, with Mallory's snow boots in his hands.

"What are you doing?" Mallory rushed toward her sister. "Get out of here!"

Eden glared at her. Eden's eyes were puffy, and strands of hair had come loose from her French twist. She brushed the hair off her wet cheeks and pointed to the center of the dresser—to another small bag of white powder and two more bags of pills.

Mallory gaped at the bags. "You found those in here?"

"We thought we'd better see what else you were hiding," Eden said. "I can't believe you stole from me."

"Stole?" Was Eden admitting the drugs were hers?

"My emergency money in my dresser," Eden said. "Two hundred and fifteen dollars. It's gone."

"I didn't take it!" The matter-of-fact mindset she'd adopted from Darien tumbled away. "These drugs aren't mine."

"Mallory, please try to stay calm." Clint spoke quietly as he set the snow boots on the carpet. If he was still angry, he hid it beneath a rational-professor mask. "Let's act like adults. No one came into your room and planted drugs."

"Yes, they did, because I *did not put them there.* And I didn't take Eden's money!"

"Don't yell," Clint said. "The neighbors don't want to be part of this."

"Let's see what's in *your* room." Mallory whirled and stalked down the hall. She expected Clint or Eden to protest, but they followed her silently.

Their normally spotless room was already a jumble.

"We searched here first," Eden said. "We also searched the living room and the kitchen, but we've already cleaned those up. Let's check your purse now." She strode toward the entryway.

Mallory pursued her. "Keep away from—"

Clint caught up to them and stepped between Mallory and Eden. Mallory wanted to shove him aside, but if she turned this into a physical confrontation, they'd take it as evidence that she was not only an addict, but also a dangerous one.

Like Nelson.

Eden opened the coat closet and retrieved Mallory's purse.

"Fine. Search it if you want," Mallory said. "There's nothing incriminating in there." Was she sure of that? Someone was setting her up. Clint? Eden? Who else could it be?

Eden rooted through the purse but only pulled out Mallory's keys. "I'll check her car."

"This is silly." Mallory started to step around Clint. With an outstretched arm, he blocked her while Eden exited.

"Sit down," he said.

"Listen to me—"

"Cooperate, or I'll call the police."

"I *wanted* to go to the police earlier. You wouldn't let me."

"I was wrong. I was thinking too much of how our friends would react, not about how much you need help. Do you want me to call the police now? I will, if that's what you want."

Mallory's tongue was paralyzed. Did she want to go to the police now and let Clint and Eden tell them her room was riddled with drugs, and Eden's money was missing?

"Sit down," Clint repeated.

Her legs shook. Trying not to tip from side to side, Mallory walked to the couch and sat down.

"Give me your phone." Standing in front of her, Clint held out his hand.

"You have no right—"

"You don't have to give it to me. But if you don't, I'm going to call the police."

Confusion deadened her brain. She couldn't face the cops when she had no idea what was going on. They wouldn't believe her. She'd get arrested.

Why would Clint or Eden set her up like this? They wouldn't. She hadn't spent much time with Eden over the last decade, but Eden was her sister. She wasn't a coldblooded devil, and Mallory had never seen evidence that Clint *wasn't* a decent man. Then again, weren't sociopaths experts at fooling people?

I've lost my mind. Sleep deprivation. Stress. Flashbacks to Mom's death after what happened to Nels.

"Your phone." Clint's voice remained steady.

She jerked her phone out of her pocket and smacked it into his palm.

"Passcode?" he asked.

Mallory recited it. Who cared if he snooped on her phone? She didn't have any secrets.

Clint stepped back and tapped the screen. Mallory assumed he was checking her texts, calls, and contacts. Hunting for her drug supplier.

The door opened, and Eden walked in. "Nothing," she said, to Mallory's relief. She'd almost expected Eden to return brandishing another baggie of drugs and claiming she'd found it in Mallory's glove box.

My own sister? She wouldn't lie about me. Clint wouldn't either. But what other explanation makes sense?

No explanation makes sense.

I need to get out of here. Now. She couldn't waste money on a hotel, but she could drive to campus, sleep in her car—anything to get away from Clint and Eden.

Mallory moved to stand. It took a moment; her limbs felt weighted. "Give me my phone and my keys. I don't know what you two are doing to me, but I'm leaving."

One of Eden's eyebrows arched. "What *we're* doing? You think we hid drugs in your room? Why would we do that?"

"I have no idea." Had Clint been using drugs to deal with work stress? Had Eden, to cope with the fact that no matter how hard she worked, she wasn't perfect? "Does one of you have a secret you want me blamed for?"

Clint and Eden both stared at her.

"Mallory," Clint began, "you're overwrought. We're all exhausted. Let's get some rest. We'll talk in the morning."

Go to bed? Talk in the morning? That's what she'd wanted when she'd arrived home, but now she only wanted to escape. "I'm leaving," she said. "Give me—"

Clint tucked her phone in his pocket while Eden closed her fist around Mallory's keys.

"You can't hold me prisoner," Mallory said.

"You're not a prisoner," Clint said. "Leave if you want, but if you go out that door tonight, I'm calling the police."

"I need my keys. I have to be to work at four."

"We know," Eden said. "We don't want you to lose your job. I'll drive you there."

"I don't need you to drive me," Mallory snapped. "I'm not under the influence of any substance except chocolate." Why was she bothering to say things she knew neither of them would believe? She probably looked anything but clean at the moment, shaking, sweating, her eyes watering.

"We'll get you in to see my doctor tomorrow," Eden said. "We'll help you through this."

"Then the doctor can test me and prove I *don't use drugs.* But I think one of you already knows that." She stumbled down the hallway and into her trashed bedroom. Her hands clumsy, she yanked the door shut and locked it.

Locked it? How would that help? Keys to the interior doors sat tidily on top of each door frame, or a bobby pin or paper clip could do the job. If she wanted to protect herself, she'd need to shove her dresser in front of the door, which was probably what Eden and Clint were doing to protect themselves from her.

She pushed a pile of clothes off her bed and slumped onto the mattress. *Stop freaking out. Think. You had a plan. Is there anything you can do tonight?*

Locks. She'd wanted to check all the exterior door and window locks for any evidence of forced entry.

Good. Give Clint and Eden time to go to sleep, then do that. You'll have to check their window in the morning, but you can check the rest of the entrances tonight. And you can check outside for footprints or other clues. The odds that she'd find any evidence were small, but knowing she could do something besides hide in her room tonight kept her stress from peaking any higher.

Hunting for clues. Good luck, Nancy Drew. Just don't get busted by Clint or Eden in the process, or you'll be chatting with the police.

CHAPTER 6

IT WAS ONE O'CLOCK IN the morning by the time Mallory felt safe slipping out of bed. For the first hour after she'd shut herself in her room, she'd listened to the muffled clicks of drawers and closets opening and closing as Eden and Clint had put their jumbled room back in order. Faint mutters of conversation that she knew centered on her had continued for another hour after the cleaning ended. She'd tried to sleep, hoping for some rest before she executed her plan, but all she ended up doing was kicking off and pulling on her covers in a game of too-hot/too-chilled and repeatedly flipping a pillow that felt hot and itchy on both sides.

She switched on her desk lamp and headed to the closet, stepping over the clothes on her floor, wishing she'd cleaned up rather than attempted to sleep. For a few seconds, she debated whether to get dressed or remain in her knit pajamas. *Pajamas, for sure.* This wouldn't take long, and maybe once she finished, she'd be able to relax enough to net an hour of sleep before she got up for work. She slid a sweatshirt off a hanger, careful not to knock the hanger against the empty hangers next to it, and put it on. Noiselessly, she slipped her feet into rubber-soled tennis shoes.

She switched off the desk lamp and shuffled across the room in the darkness to open her door, grateful the hinges didn't creak. She stepped into the hallway and eased the door shut. Trailing her fingers along the wall to guide herself, she tiptoed to the kitchen.

Moonlight streaming through the windows lit the kitchen so she could navigate it without bumping into anything. From the pantry, she took the flashlight from its wall bracket, her hands already sweaty and her heartbeat sprinting. *Take a deep breath. Even if you get caught, maybe Clint won't call the police on you. I mean, it's not suspicious or creepy for a drug-addicted liar to slink around your house in the middle of the night, examining doorknobs and latches.*

Clint might know full well the drugs weren't hers anyway.

Moving with small, slow steps, she headed for the front door. The soft clanking noises involved in unbolting the deadbolt and turning the doorknob seemed to echo like she'd banged a hammer against a cast-iron pot. *Stay calm. Eden and Clint are in their bedroom at the other end of the house. They won't hear you unlocking a door.*

The furnace clicked on, generating a whoosh of warm air through the vents, but otherwise, the house remained silent. Mallory edged the door open a few inches and shone the flashlight along the door jamb. Smooth, unchipped paint and wood. She studied the metal strike plate and the bolt itself. Maybe an expert could see something she couldn't, but there was no obvious damage. She drew the door open a little wider and slipped through the opening so she stood on the porch. Bringing her face close to the locks—*where's your magnifying glass, Nancy?*—she studied the keyholes for the deadbolt and the knob. No weird or fresh scratches.

A fraction of an inch at a time, she pulled the door closed behind her. Relieved to have a door and exterior walls now muting any noise she might make, she hurried down the porch steps and veered behind the bushes so she could examine the living room window and the area around it. No footprint-style dents in the mulch. No damage to the lower part of the frame that suggested someone had pried at or forced anything. If she wanted to examine the whole window, she'd need a stepstool to reach the top. Was it worth creeping back into the house to get a stool? The top of the window probably didn't have any suspicious marks. Then again, she had no idea how to break in through a window like this—there *could* be evidence there for all she knew. *Get the stepstool. Don't do half the job and quit. That won't help.*

Cold wind ruffled her hair and hit her sweaty neck like a slosh of ice water. Annoyed that she hadn't thought to bring the stool with her in the first place, she started toward the front door.

Back inside, she stepped gingerly across the wood floor toward the pantry, fighting a sense that she'd exhausted the floor's tolerance for stealth and this time it would creak in places it hadn't before.

The floorboards didn't creak. She made it into the pantry, where she retrieved the folded stepstool. Back through the dark living room, out the front door, and finally she was on track again. Sweatier and shakier than before, she finished checking the window, picked up the stool, and hurried to the next window.

How could a yard full of trees so pretty that they belonged on a "Birch Falls in autumn" stock photo look like a haunted forest at night? Mallory kept glancing over her shoulder and squinting between moonlit tree trunks. She didn't dare sweep her flashlight beam around the yard. The more she waved the light around, the more likely she'd attract attention from neighbors—neighbors who would call the police to report a burglar.

She hurried up the steps of the back deck, wincing when the wood *did* creak. *Relax. They won't hear it inside.* She set the stool next to her and bent to scrutinize the back doorknob. The flashlight beam glinted off unscratched brass. She couldn't open the door to check the doorjamb; Eden had her keys. She should have taken the spare keys off the rack that hung on the side of the fridge. Now she'd have to—

A crunching-rustling to the left of the deck set fire to her nerves. She whirled to look in that direction, stabbing the flashlight beam between trees. Nothing. *Don't get spooked by branches and wind.* Hastily she re-aimed the beam at the door to search for any nicks in the wood near the doorknob. No visible damage. She picked up the stepstool and started toward the family room window that opened onto the deck.

A barky cry made her jump and whack herself in the shin with a leg of the stool. A wild animal—maybe a wolf or a stray dog. The cry came again, from overhead. *That's not a bark. It's a bird noise. Some kind of owl, maybe. Nothing that's going to attack you.* Gritting her teeth, she continued toward the window, checked it, and hastened down the steps of the deck, wanting to check the other side of the house as quickly as she could.

As she rounded the corner of the house, rhythmic rustles came from behind her. She dropped the stool and spun around, arcing the flashlight beam around her.

A maple leaf drifted to the ground, spotlighted by the beam. *No one's out here. You're such a wimp.*

Heart pounding, she picked up the stool and all but ran toward the next window, determined not to run all the way to the front door and lock herself inside. *Finish, finish, finish. There's nothing out here except owls and trees. Whoever hid the drugs isn't hanging around 24/7 stalking you.*

She planted the stepstool in the mulch and climbed onto the first step.

Rustling noises. One after the other, drawing closer. Mallory leapt to the ground, not even looking behind her, grabbed the stepstool, and sprinted for the front door. With no effort to be stealthy, she leaped up the porch steps, yanked the door open, and raced inside. Only as she went to shut the door did she catch herself and manage to close it quietly. She locked it, pulled off her tennis shoes and speed-walked barefoot toward her bedroom, the beam of the flashlight illuminating the hallway.

Clint and Eden's door remained shut and Mallory heard no footsteps or voices from inside their bedroom. In her room, she closed and locked her door and set the stepstool down, boggled that she'd instinctively snatched it before fleeing. Even when scared silly, her brain apparently didn't want to annoy Eden by leaving the stool outside.

She switched off the flashlight, crumbled to the floor, and leaned against the door. Had that been Clint outside? Had it been anyone at all? She closed her eyes, listening for sounds of someone reentering the house.

The sounds didn't come.

CHAPTER 7

AT TWO-THIRTY IN THE morning, Mallory finally flopped onto her bed and dozed. At three-fifteen, her alarm startled her awake. Before showering, she returned the flashlight and stepstool to the pantry. When she looked outside, the yard didn't seem ominous now—just as dark and deserted as it always was when she left for work. She shouldn't have let her imagination go wild last night.

While Mallory was standing in front of the hallway mirror drying her hair, Eden emerged from her bedroom. She didn't ask questions about middle-of-the-night disturbances; she merely set Mallory's phone on the dressing table and quietly mentioned that it was fully charged. Trust Eden to plug it in before going to bed. She didn't return Mallory's keys, and Mallory didn't bother to demand them, nor did she bother avoiding Eden's searching looks in the mirror. Lack of sleep had rendered Mallory glassy-eyed and pale, which Eden would no doubt regard as signs of drug use or withdrawal.

"Would you like anything to eat?" Eden asked. "We have the last of that cinnamon bread I made on Monday. Or I could make you a cup of hibiscus tea."

"No, thank you. I'll eat later."

They didn't speak as Eden drove Mallory to campus. When Mallory was exiting the car at the Rains Building, Eden said, "I'll call you as soon as I talk to the doctor."

Mallory nodded and shut the door. She wanted to talk to Darien about last night, but she'd have to wait a few hours. He'd planned to come in when she finished at eight to take her to breakfast. She couldn't call him now, waking him up, whimpering and accusing her family of turning against her.

Darien showed up at seven forty-five. Mallory wheeled the vacuum into the janitorial closet, so tired it was hard not to steer it into the walls. Darien hurried toward her.

"I'm sorry," he said. "You look exhausted. I kept you up too late, didn't I?"

"It's not that. I couldn't sleep. Things are a disaster. Come talk to me while I clean the drinking fountains. Then I'm finished."

When they reached the first drinking fountain, Darien took the spray cleaner out of her hand. "Let me."

She ripped a paper towel off the roll, handed it to him, and told her story while he worked.

"I feel like I'm losing my mind," she said after she'd finished her report. "First I accuse Clint and Eden to their faces—my own family—then I go creeping around the yard in the middle of the night and convince myself I'm about to . . . about to . . . I don't even know. Get stabbed or get eaten by a werewolf or something." Mallory handed Darien a fresh paper towel. "This is such a mess. I can't believe Clint or Eden would do this to me, but who else could it be? I hardly know anyone in Birch Falls. I've only been here a month and a half. How could I have made an enemy who'd want to frame me?"

"You're certain *you're* the target?" Darien polished the handle of the fountain. "Maybe there are drugs throughout the house and the culprit wants all of you in trouble."

"They searched the whole house, or said they did. The only places they found drugs were in Eden's makeup drawer and in my bedroom."

As they walked toward the next drinking fountain, Mallory kept awkwardly bumping her hand or elbow into Darien. She veered a step away from him. Was the part of her brain that controlled personal space still asleep? *Maybe you just want to hold his hand. Or you can't walk straight due to imaginary drug use.*

Darien sprayed cleaner on the drinking fountain. "If Clint or Eden has a drug problem, maybe that person got scared the spouse was catching on and tried to divert suspicion by blaming you."

"I don't *know*. They've been a huge help to me, and besides, it doesn't make sense. If one of them has an ongoing drug problem, there must be money besides Eden's emergency cash that's unaccounted for, but they didn't say anything about that. Eden keeps such careful track of her money; she would have noticed anything missing. Maybe Clint is planning to claim there's been money missing from his wallet?"

"Seems like he would have mentioned that last night," Darien said.

"After they found the drugs in my room, they took my keys and my phone and warned me that if I left, they'd call the police. You'd think the guilty one of them would have tried to kick me out before their scheme could fall apart, rather than pretending they're worried about me. They both seem on board with taking me to the doctor, but they must know the first thing I'll do is insist on a drug test, and that will prove I haven't—"

Suddenly lightheaded, Mallory stopped. She'd assumed a doctor-supervised test would at least prove she hadn't used drugs recently, but what if it didn't? She often ate Eden's cooking—what if Eden had been slipping tiny amounts of . . .

Are you kidding?

Mallory sat on the tile floor of the hall and pressed her burning eyes against her bent knees. Footsteps, a soft thump, and fabric brushing her arm told her Darien had sat next to her. He laid his hand on her shoulder. "Mallory?"

She kept her head lowered. "I'm crazy paranoid. I'm seriously losing it." *How can I suspect my own family? Then again, they suspect me. More than suspect. They're sure I'm guilty.*

"Hey, let's stick with the original plan, all right?" Darien's fingers massaged her shoulder. His touch calmed her, and within a few moments, her anxiety started to erode, washed out by sleepiness.

"The fact that the situation is worse than we thought doesn't change how we approach it." Darien's hand shifted and began to rub the knotted muscles in her other shoulder. "We need to find out if anyone's been seen near your sister's house."

"Besides me creeping around at one in the morning?" A few more minutes of Darien's comforting touch and she'd conk out with her head on her knees. She wanted him to reassure her that he believed the drugs weren't hers, but that wasn't a fair expectation. She and Darien had barely become friends. He didn't know her that well.

This was pathetic. It had been so long since she'd been interested in a guy, and how did she start off? By playing the role of a needy, hysterical, possibly unstable, probably drug-addicted drama queen. Whatever smidgen of romantic interest he'd had in her when he'd brought her the flowers must have evaporated during this morning's paranoid rant.

"You okay?" Darien asked.

She lifted her head and tried to smile. "Just really, really tired. And confused."

Darien rested his hand on her back. "Is there any other way Eden or Clint could benefit from getting you in trouble—besides setting you up to hide their own issues?"

"Yes. If they can make it appear I died of an overdose, Eden inherits my share of the family diamonds and gets total control of our gold mine."

He grinned. "A solid motive at last."

"Sorry." Mallory laughed weakly. "I'm not used to acting like a character in a PBS Mystery special. No, I don't have any money, or I wouldn't be working a four-in-the-morning janitorial job and taking out student loans to pay for school. We don't have any rich relatives. Our parents had more debts than assets. Uncle Mike doesn't have much money, and anything he does have will go to his sons, not me. I don't own anything valuable. My car is sixteen years old and smells like Pine-Sol. I shop at thrift stores." She pointed to her Bowman University sweatshirt. "I bought this at Goodwill for six dollars."

"Could they be after something other than money?"

"Nothing." She rested her head against the wall behind her.

"What time is your first class? Do you have time for a nap?"

"My class isn't until ten, but even if I had my car, I wouldn't want to go home." *This is ridiculous. Eden's going to call me about a doctor appointment, and I have no idea what to tell her. I can't believe I don't trust my own family, and they don't trust me.*

What's wrong with us?

"How about this?" Darien rose and reached down to help her to her feet. "First, let me get you some breakfast. Then I know the perfect place where you can take a nap. My advisor is in Chicago, presenting at a conference, and I have a key to his office. There's a couch in there. It's private and quiet. Nobody's going to bother you."

"If I lie down, I'm afraid I'll sleep right through my class."

"That's okay."

Sleep through one class . . . sleep through another . . . hide in a fog of oblivion. Deeper panic stirred inside her. "It's isn't okay. Darien, I can't."

"Do you have something in class you can't make up later?"

"That doesn't matter." She grabbed the sleeve of his sweater. "I can't skip, I can't do that."

"Mallory, take it easy."

"I can't backslide!"

"Backslide?"

"I'll end up like I was before, when everything fell apart."

He touched her hand. "Missing one class under extreme circumstances is not backsliding."

"Maybe not, but . . . Then again, everything *is* falling apart. I'll miss all the classes when I get kicked out."

"You're not going to get kicked out."

"I think I am. I think I'm going to jail."

"How about you nap for a little while? You can't tackle problems effectively when you're hungry and exhausted."

Mallory retrieved the roll of paper towels and the bottle of spray cleaner and started toward the stairwell.

"Are you planning to take those with you?" Darien asked.

"What?"

"The janitorial closet is in the other direction."

"Right." Mallory halted. "I should put these away. And I need to get my coat. No, I didn't wear a coat. Just the sweatshirt. Wait, I think I wore a coat."

"We'll check." With his hand on her elbow, Darien steered her toward the closet.

"I don't want to see Eden's doctor," Mallory said.

"Let's find someone else, a doctor with no connection to your sister."

Mallory swallowed. Her mouth was parched. She should have gotten a drink before she'd walked away from the fountain. "I'm afraid to see anyone until I know what's going on."

"Isn't it a doctor's job to help you figure out what's going on? You wanted to get a drug test."

Mallory feared that saying *but what if Eden has been slipping me something* would sound so paranoid that Darien might drive her straight to the ER. Instead, she defaulted to the excuse he'd offered her a moment ago. "I'm too tired to think this through."

"Agreed."

"I'll take a short nap." Mallory yawned. "Maybe half an hour."

"That's a start," Darien said.

CHAPTER 8

AFTER HIS ELEVEN O'CLOCK CLASS, Darien left the classroom with no idea what the discussion had been about. How could he help Mallory? As far as he knew, she was still sleeping in Dr. Agosto's office. Earlier this morning, when the alarm she'd insisted on setting had beeped, she'd fumbled to cancel it, peered fuzzily at Darien, sitting at Agosto's desk, and muttered, "I'll get up in a minute." An hour later, she was still deeply asleep, and Darien had had no inclination to wake her. He'd left her a note to call him as soon as she woke up and crept out of the office.

Now what? He'd reviewed and analyzed everything she'd told him. He'd input it all into a spreadsheet: what had happened, at what time, how Mallory interpreted each event, what Clint and Eden had said—as reported by Mallory—and his own thoughts.

He didn't have enough information.

As he crossed campus, he debated what to do. Finally, he conceded that seeking out the other side of the story was better than hunkering down in his cubicle, uselessly wishing he knew more. This might be a mistake that would destroy his friendship with Mallory, but it was the most productive option he could think of, the clearest way to move forward. He checked the faculty directory and dialed the number for Dr. Clinton Westcott.

Voice mail. Darien cleared his throat and spoke. "Hi, my name is Darien Thomas. I'm a friend of your sister-in-law, Mallory Ingram, and wanted to talk to you about her." He recited his number and hung up, slightly relieved that he had more time to think about what to ask Clint.

As he sat down in his cubicle, his phone rang. The number on the screen was the one he'd just called, and it provoked a sudden case of cold feet. He wrestled against the temptation to let the call go to voice mail. *Don't lose your nerve, idiot. Answer it.* "Hello?"

"This is Clint Westcott, returning your call."

"Thanks for calling me back. I was speaking to Mallory this morning—"

"Do you know where she is?" Clint interrupted. "My wife and I have been trying to get in touch with her."

Darien wasn't ready to share that he did know Mallory's location. "Sir, I'd like to talk to you about that, but could we meet in person?"

"Are you near campus?"

"Yes."

"I'm free right now if you can come to my office. It's number 450 in the Yarborough Center."

Praying that Mallory would forgive him for seeking information from her accuser, he said, "I'll be there in five minutes."

The sky was overcast, and wind ripped leaves from the trees as Darien walked toward the Yarborough Center. On the fourth floor, he found Clint Westcott's office. The door was open, and Clint stood to welcome him.

"Thanks for contacting me." Clint was a sharp-dressed guy with a baby face, the type that would look young even when he had ten grandkids. He appeared tired, though not as exhausted as Mallory.

"Thanks for meeting with me," Darien said.

"Close the door and have a seat." Clint sat in the chair behind his desk. "What led you to call me about Mallory?"

"Well, last night and this morning, she told me some disturbing things." Darien took care not to sound accusatory. "I'd like to hear your perspective."

"What did she say?"

"I'd appreciate hearing your side of the story first, if you don't mind."

Clint's pleasant expression went flat. "I take it you've come to defend her."

"I want to help her. Until I understand the situation completely, I have no idea how to do that."

"If you want to help her, we're on the same page. What I'm telling you is completely confidential. I hope, for Mallory's sake, you'll keep it that way."

Darien nodded.

"Mallory has a drug problem," Clint said. "We found out yesterday and tried to talk to her about it, but she was defensive and hostile."

Darien tried to keep his voice neutral. "What evidence did you find of drug use?"

"Drugs hidden in her room. And she's stolen money from Eden. Her sister. My wife."

"She's stolen money? Are you certain it was Mallory?"

Clint's eyes scrutinized Darien as keenly as Darien was scrutinizing Clint. "During the period in which the money went missing, Mallory was the only one who could have taken it."

"You're sure?"

"Yes. Eden knows the money was there three days ago when she took out twenty dollars. No one has visited our home since then."

"How secure is your house? Do you have a security system?"

"There was no evidence of a break-in. Even if a thief managed to enter without leaving any signs, why would he leave jewelry and electronics behind and take the cash without disturbing anything else?"

"Fair enough," Darien said. "What evidence of drug use have you seen in Mallory?"

Clint straightened a framed picture on his desk. Darien couldn't see who was in the picture; he assumed it was Eden. "We don't see much of Mallory, so she's been able to hide most of the signs. But we've seen bloodshot eyes, excessive tiredness, isolation, secretiveness, paranoia."

Excessive tiredness? She has to be to work at 4:00 a.m. I'd look tired too on that schedule. "Secretiveness?" Darien asked.

"If she's home, she's in her room, or she heads there the instant I walk through the door. She seems intent on staying out of sight."

"What signs of paranoia does she show?"

Clint fiddled with a bowl displaying four tennis-ball sized objects wrapped in different patterns of colored thread. "Making accusations against her sister and me, accusing us of holding her prisoner, of trying to frame her."

"So this 'paranoia' manifested itself after you found the drugs? Not before?"

"She also has a history," Clint said.

"Of drug use?"

Clint picked up one of the balls, a white one with a blue and brown pattern, and rolled it between his palms. "It's not completely clear what she was involved in, but she hung with a bad crowd."

"She told me about that. That was several years ago."

"Which doesn't render it irrelevant now." Clint dropped the white ball into the bowl and picked up one with a pattern in orange, red, and yellow.

"Those are interesting creations," Darien commented.

Clint tossed the ball to him. "What does that remind you of?"

Darien rotated it, impressed by the intricate and precise patterns of thread. "It's a . . . spherical truncated icosahedron."

Clint chuckled. "That one is autumn." He picked up the white ball. "This is winter." He picked up the other two balls. "Spring and summer. It's a good thing Eden didn't hear your answer, because she gets irritated that no one recognizes the theme here."

"She makes these?"

"Yes. Temari, a Japanese art. I told her if she wants the people visiting my office to appreciate her themes, she ought to decorate her next temari with a relational object database mapping diagram."

Darien grinned and tossed the temari ball to Clint. "Tell her I'm impressed with her skill and appreciate her four-seasons theme, even if I didn't clue into it."

Clint returned the autumn temari to the bowl. "I realize that as Mallory's friend, you want to defend her, but denial will only hurt her. If her drug use comes to the attention of the police and the university, she'll get arrested and expelled. Mallory has had enough trouble getting herself to this point. If you care about her, help us help her before she destroys her life."

"I want to help her," Darien said. "That's why I'm talking to you. But all this evidence is circumstantial. I've never seen signs that Mallory uses drugs. Until last night, all I've seen is . . ." He thought about his early morning chats with Mallory. "A woman who is hardworking, smart, friendly, funny, conscientious—" *Stop talking, nerd. You've already made it obvious you're crushing on her.*

"Then where did the drugs come from?" Clint asked. "She agreed to let Eden set up a doctor appointment for her, but now she's refusing to take Eden's calls. Why would she avoid seeing a doctor if she's clean?"

"Maybe because she *is* clean and seeing a doctor would be a waste of time." Darien scanned the bookshelves. It was easier to focus on the spines of books on computational theory, JavaScript, and MySQL than to meet Clint's eyes and see frustration and anxiety. Clint seemed reasonable. Concerned for Mallory.

Darien had left his sweater with Mallory, but even in his short sleeves, he felt overheated. He wanted to believe her. But did he have any reason—any rational reason—for believing her over Clint Westcott? Incontestably, Clint's interpretation made more sense than Mallory's confused insistence that she'd been set up.

"You said you've spoken to her today," Clint said. "How is she?"

Darien rallied. It was time to shove back and see how Clint reacted. "Scared to death, trying to figure out why someone would do this to her. Is there any possibility someone in your household is trying to cover up their own issues by blaming them on Mallory? Have there been problems before this? Other money missing, maybe from your bank account?"

"My wife would never do anything like this. I would never do anything like this, and we never experienced any problems before Mallory moved in."

"Do you or your wife have any enemies? Maybe someone is trying to hurt you through Mallory."

"No. And Eden checked with our neighbors. They haven't noticed anyone around our house."

"She checked?"

"Yes, this morning. It was a long shot, but do you think she *wants* to believe her sister is using drugs? If you care about Mallory, get her to talk to us and see a doctor. Do you know where she is right now? She skipped her class this morning."

"You went searching for her?"

"I told you, I'm trying to help her. Do you know where she is?"

Darien debated whether it was time to answer that question.

"I won't drag her to the police, or to a doctor," Clint said. "At least, not today. We just want to talk to her, but she's ignoring our messages. Will you help us get in touch with her? Or do you believe her accusation that we're planting drugs in her room?"

"It's not really an accusation," Darien said. "It's panicked brainstorming. She's struggling to figure out what happened."

"I understand why she's having trouble facing this. Of course it's scary for her, and, frankly, we were so upset last night that we were on the attack. If I could talk to her now, I may be able to calm things down between us."

Darien hesitated. *How can I best help Mallory?*

Not by helping her hide.

"I'll talk to her," he said. "I'll do everything I can to convince her to meet with you and your wife, but let me approach her alone first. If I send you straight to her, she'll lose whatever trust she has in me—if she has any left—and that won't help us sort this out."

"Good plan." Clint stood and extended his hand. "Talk to her. Then call me."

Darien reluctantly shook Clint's hand, discouraged that the only thing he'd learned from the meeting was that he had no compelling reasons for believing Mallory. "I'll be in touch."

"Thank you." Clint walked him to the door and reached for the knob, but he didn't pull the door open. For an awkward few seconds, Darien waited.

Clint's brow creased, and he dropped his hand from the knob. "One last thing," he said. "Do you know if Mallory has used the spare house keys lately?"

"The spare house keys?" Darien thought of Mallory's story of creeping around outside in the middle of the night. She'd mentioned that she hadn't had keys with her. "You mean 'lately' as in yesterday?"

"Lately as in the past week or two."

"I don't know. She told me Eden took her keys, but she didn't say anything about using spare keys. Are they missing?"

"No. Will you ask her if she's used them? Or even moved them or knocked them off the key rack? If she's handled them at all?"

"Sure. Why—"

"It's not likely to be relevant. But ask her."

"Yeah, sure, I'll do that."

"Thanks." Clint opened the door. "I'll speak with you soon."

CHAPTER 9

HUDDLED ON THE COUCH IN Dr. Agosto's office, Mallory gripped her phone, her thumbs hovering over the screen as she tried to convince herself to answer Eden's texts. Eden's messages had started out matter-of-fact, had turned curt, and now sounded pleading.

Mallory wanted to collapse, rest her head on Darien's folded sweater, and plunge back into sleep.

Don't do it. You need to take care of this.

A key clicked in the lock, and Darien stepped into the office. "Got your text," he said. "I'm glad you were able to sleep. Feeling any better?"

Mallory nodded. Darien's hair was mussed, probably thanks to the blustery wind that kept blowing leaves against the window of the office.

He sat on the couch next to her. "Ready for lunch?"

She was hungry, but exiting the office sounded like a trek too difficult to begin. *Skipping class, burrowing in an absent professor's office.* She was sinking right back to where she'd been, unable to cope, mentally trapped.

When she didn't say anything, Darien spoke quietly. "Mallory, listen. I . . . talked to your brother-in-law."

Jolted, she gaped at him. "Clint contacted you? How did he know—"

"I contacted him." Scarlet patches formed on his neck. "I wanted to help you."

Mallory sagged against the back of the couch. "You think I'm lying to you."

"I went to Clint hoping to get information. Not because I think you're lying."

"What did he say?"

"Essentially the same things you told me. He interprets them differently, but you're sharing the same facts. He seems sincerely worried about you." Darien's dark eyes were kind but intensely focused as he met her gaze. "I'll be candid with you. I have no idea what's going on here. I haven't made up my mind about anything—I still don't have enough information. But I *am* your friend, and I want to help you. Clint wants to talk to you. I told him I'd try to convince you to do that."

The sense that she was alone in dark mist stirred panic. Darien had talked to Clint. Darien believed Clint, not her.

No. Darien hadn't said that. He'd said he didn't know what to think. "Thank you for telling me the truth."

"I'm sorry if you feel I betrayed you by talking to him."

She shook her head. "I want you to believe me. But if you flat-out believed me without question, considering the evidence piled against me, you'd be an idiot."

His platinum brows rose. "You honestly feel that way?"

Mallory smiled bleakly. "If you knew me well and doubted me, *that* would really hurt, but you don't. And if you're a guy who'll keep blindly defending a near-stranger even when all the evidence says I may be a toxic liar—that's not chivalrous; that's dumb. What matters to me is that you're keeping your mind open and you want to help me."

"I do." The relief in his smile eased her sense of isolation. He'd gone to Clint because he cared about her. "For a moment, let's assume you're innocent and Clint and Eden are too. He claims Eden checked with the neighbors, but they haven't seen anything suspicious."

Mallory wasn't sure if Eden genuinely had checked, but the possibility made her hopeful. "I was going to do that this morning, but after my haunted-forest escapade last night, I got scared that the only thing they'd report seeing was me."

"Clint didn't mention that, so apparently no one noticed you."

"Did he say *he* followed me around the yard in the dark?"

"Didn't mention that either."

Mallory sighed. "Because he probably didn't. No one did."

Darien opened his backpack and took out the bag of chocolate-covered pretzels he'd purchased at the chocolate shop the night before. He passed it to her.

"Thanks." Mallory unfastened the twist-tie around the bag and took out a pretzel.

"Clint wanted me to ask you if you've used the spare house keys lately," Darien said.

Mallory crunched her final bite of pretzel and reached for another one. "You mean, did I take them after Eden confiscated my keys? No."

"He was more general than that. He wanted to know if you'd used them or even handled them over the past few weeks."

"Why?"

"He didn't say."

"They're lost?"

"No. He said they weren't missing."

"I haven't done anything with them." Was Clint afraid she had let her drug supplier use the keys for in-home delivery?

"Where are the keys kept?" Darien asked.

"There's a board with key hooks on the side of the fridge. A Pinteresty creation of Eden's. That's where all the keys go."

"Hmm." Darien leaned back and stretched out his long legs. "When we talk to Clint, we'll find out why he wanted to know. Right now, let's widen the range for brainstorming. You said you don't know anyone well enough to make an enemy here. Maybe we need to look further back. I apologize for bringing this up, but you told me a drug addict killed your mother. Is there anything related to that incident that could lead someone to target you now?"

"He's dead." A knot hurt Mallory's throat, and she set the pretzel bag down. "He was killed during a prison riot a couple of weeks ago. That time you saw me crying at work—my uncle had just called to give me the news."

"A couple of weeks ago?" Darien sat up straight and gave her a thoughtful look. "I'm sorry. His death must have stirred everything up. Reminded you of what he did to your mother."

"Yes, but I was also sad for *him.* He didn't mean to kill her, and he was devastated at what he'd done. Nelson was a—a friend of mine. I was the one who—" Memory flamed, charring her.

Darien grasped her hand. "You were the one who what?"

Tears spilled down her face. "I was the one who gave him the idea to target my house. It was at an awful party . . . I threw it when my mom was on a weekend getaway with friends. Things happened at the party that I shouldn't have allowed. Nelson brought drugs, and so did a few other friends. I should have thrown them out. Instead I joked about how my mom would never suspect, that she was so naive, acted like we were living in a cute little farm town in 1910. The kind of trusting person who hardly ever bothered to lock her car or the front door . . ." Mallory's chest heaved; she fought to breathe steadily. The flames spread.

Darien's arms enveloped her. She slumped against him and let herself sob. Spilling tears was a familiar sensation, but spilling them onto someone's shoulder was not, and the bony warmth of Darien's shoulder made it easy to release the rest of the story.

"That's why Nelson chose our house—because he knew it would be easy to get in. He was desperate for money . . . already owed his dealer, needed his next fix . . . He knew my mom volunteered at the library on Wednesday nights and I always went with her to study there. But she'd stayed home that night to rest; she had a headache. The lights were off, and I'd taken the car to the grocery store, so Nelson didn't realize anyone was home. She walked in on him when he was stuffing her laptop into his bag. He panicked. Swung a lamp that hit her in the head. She fell and hit her head a second time. I . . . came home just as . . . as Nelson was running away. She died of a brain hemorrhage later that night."

"I'm so sorry." Darien stroked her hair. "Mallory, what Nelson chose to do is not your fault."

"I know," she sobbed. "But I was stupid, and the result was . . . I'm sorry. I thought I was handling this. I *did* eventually go to counseling."

"I doubt counseling comes with a guarantee that traumatic events will never hurt again," Darien said gently.

"But I'm *not* using illegal drugs to deal with this. Do you see why I would *never*—after what happened to Mom—"

Darien lifted his arms from around her and shifted so he was facing her. "This is going to be a painful question, but we need to explore it. Did Nelson's family know the details of what happened? Why he chose your house?"

"Yes." She wiped her face on the sleeve of her sweatshirt. "I don't know if Nelson told them, but his lawyer talked about it at the plea bargain. He argued that Nelson was a good kid—well, a good young man;

he was eighteen—who'd been overwhelmed by irresistible temptation and deserved leniency."

"Did he ever hint that it was your fault? Like you'd lured Nelson there?"

Mallory thought back. "He didn't directly blame me, but he did make it clear that the party I'd thrown and the information I'd given Nelson when he was at a vulnerable point were the catalyst for his crimes." Sobs that had begun to ebb threatened to spike again. She reached instinctively for Darien's hand. "Mind if . . . I . . . hold onto you?"

"Please do." He held her hand with both of his. "Did Nelson's family blame you?"

"I don't know." She drew a deep breath. "They never confronted me. You're suggesting they could be the ones planting the drugs now, trying to get revenge by getting me in trouble?"

"Just a thought. If they believe Nelson never would have ended up in prison if you hadn't given him the idea to break into your house, maybe they feel you deserve it."

Mallory tried to picture Nelson's family coming after her. "This happened five years ago and three thousand miles away. If they blamed me, why wouldn't they have taken revenge at the time . . . Never mind. I see what you're saying. Maybe it took his death to get them hating me this much. Could you hand me those tissues?"

Darien released her hand, stood, and grabbed the box of tissues from Dr. Agosto's desk. "What's his family like?"

"Serious problems. Thanks." Mallory accepted the tissues. "His mom was abusive. His dad was an addict. He's the one who got Nels hooked. His dad died of an overdose a few months after Nelson was arrested. Nelson had a sister, Lori, who was . . . um . . . two years older. He adored her. Super smart but made a lot of dumb decisions. I can relate."

"Do you know where his mother and Lori are now?"

"No." Mallory couldn't imagine Nelson's mother tracking her down, following her across the country, and sneaking into Clint and Eden's house. She wouldn't be patient enough for that. If she came after Mallory, it would be to scream at her and punch her.

But what about Lori?

"It's far-fetched, but so is everything else," Mallory said. "I'll call my uncle to see if he knows anything about what Lori Sanders is up to."

CHAPTER 10

CLINT WAVED MALLORY AND DARIEN into his office. "Thank you for coming."

Eden sprang to her feet then hesitated. Shadows showed through the concealer under her eyes, and her linen jacket hung crooked. Mallory scanned the jacket and realized the buttons weren't in the correct buttonholes. That was a first for Eden. And she must have left work early. Another first.

"I'm sorry," Mallory said. "I should have answered your texts."

Eden took a halting step forward and wrapped her arms around Mallory. Mallory hugged her back. To Mallory's surprise, Eden didn't let go, but cinched her arms so tightly she all but deflated Mallory's lungs.

"Mal." Eden's voice broke. "I'm so sorry. I've been horrible to you. Horrible for years."

"What are you talking about? That's not true."

Eden drew back, tears flooding from her eyes. "I hardly kept in touch with you after I moved out, and when Mom died, I left you to deal with it on your own. You were still a kid, and I didn't even bother to—"

Mallory's tear-achy eyes filled again. "I didn't expect you to—You had a life away from—"

"You expected me to *abandon* you? Leave you with our old uncle who didn't have a clue?"

"Uncle Mike did his best—"

"I know he meant well, and he tried, but how long did it take him to realize how bad things were and to get you help?" Eden wiped her eyes.

"Of course, he did a lot better than I did. What did *I* do to help? Text you a couple of times a week to ask if you were getting out of the house or to tell you to find some better friends or go to school."

"Eden—"

"No wonder you don't trust me to help you now." Eden clamped her hands on Mallory's shoulders. "I *will* help you."

Clint put his arm around Eden's waist. "Let's sit down and hear what Mallory has to say."

Eden released her. Dazed, Mallory sank into the nearest chair. Eden pulled a chair close and linked arms with Mallory so their shoulders touched. Mallory wasn't sure if Eden wanted to comfort her or prevent her from escaping, but the sisterly contact was soothing.

"Darien, you're welcome to . . ." Clint gestured toward the only remaining chair in his office, his desk chair.

"Thank you, Dr. Westcott, but I'll stand."

Clint sat; Darien stood next to Mallory.

Stay calm, Mallory told herself. *No matter what anyone says, you can stay calm.* "I understand why you think I have a drug problem," she said. "But I don't, so I'm trying to figure out what's going on." She explained what she and Darien had discussed about the Sanders family. Clint leaned forward while he listened, arms on his desk, gaze sharp.

"I talked to Uncle Mike," Mallory continued. "I told him what's been happening here and asked if he'd heard any rumors about the Sanders family blaming me for Nelson's death. Uncle Mike told me that the day after Nelson's funeral, someone threw a rock through his living room window."

Eden gasped. "Through Uncle Mike's window?"

Mallory nodded. "There was other vandalism too. Mom's grave."

Eden's fingernails speared Mallory's arm. "What happened to it?"

"Graffiti. Profanity, mainly. Mike wouldn't tell me exactly what it said, but the idea was that Mom deserved to die."

"That's *horrible.* Why didn't he tell us this before?"

"He said there'd been no point in worrying us."

"Oh, Mike." Eden sighed. "The silent stoic."

"Do the police think Lori Sanders is responsible?" Clint asked.

"Uncle Mike said he mentioned the Sanders family to the police as people who might have a grudge against us, but he never heard of any arrests. One of the Sanderses' neighbors is in the chess club with Uncle Mike, so at their meeting, Uncle Mike asked this lady about the family. She told him that a few days after the funeral, Lori had left town along with her newest boyfriend—who has served time for drug dealing."

"What about Nelson's mother?" Eden asked.

"She's been threatening to sue the state for negligence in Nelson's death. She's also been complaining about Lori abandoning her."

Clint tapped his fingers on his desk, lips pursed. "If crude vandalism is Lori's style, would she have the patience to attempt to frame you? Why not break *our* window?"

"Maybe the thuggish stuff is her boyfriend's style," Mallory guessed. "Nelson used to tell me how clever Lori was—devious. Maybe she wants more satisfaction than a smashed window and nasty words on a gravestone."

"Getting you busted for possession, thrown out of school, maybe sent to jail?" Clint picked up one of Eden's temari balls from the bowl on his desk. "If the police in Gilroy suspect Lori is on a vengeful rampage, it would have been nice of them to warn you."

"It sounds like they couldn't tie anything to her, and it probably didn't occur to them that she'd travel to the opposite coast to harass me."

Neither Clint nor Eden spoke. Mallory suspected they were thinking that it hadn't occurred to them because it was a ridiculous theory.

"I want to go to the Birch Falls police," Mallory said. "But I'm nervous asking them to investigate whether Lori Sanders is in town while you two are insisting the drugs you found are mine."

"We don't want to blame you for something you're innocent of." The wariness in Clint's tone made it obvious to Mallory that he was thinking, "You're still as likely a suspect as Lori."

"Where are the drugs now?" Darien asked.

"I put them in my safe," Clint said. "We can give them to the police."

Eden squeezed Mallory's arm. "If there's an outside explanation for how they ended up in our house, let's find it."

At least Eden and Clint were willing to question Mallory's guilt. That was the most she could hope for. "All right," Mallory said. "Let's call the police."

"Dr. Westcott, you were asking about the spare keys," Darien said. "Mallory hasn't used or handled them recently. Why did you want to know that?"

"Oh, the keys." Under his palm, Clint rolled the ball along the desk. "It probably isn't significant, but—"

"—they were on the wrong hook," Eden said, a flare of realization in her eyes. "I forgot about that. A week or so ago."

"The wrong hook?" Darien asked.

"There's a board with hooks for keys on the side of our fridge. Each key has its own hook. They're labeled. The spare keys were hanging on the 'house keys' hook instead of the 'spare house keys' hook."

Darien blinked. "Is that a . . . weird occurrence?"

Mallory bit her lip, figuring now wasn't a good time to giggle.

"It's weird if all of us deny having touched the spare keys in the recent past." Clint pressed the thread-wrapped ball between his palms. "Which we all have."

"Clint, those aren't stress balls," Eden said.

"Sorry." Clint returned the ball to the bowl.

Mallory contemplated the mis-hung keys. "Maybe an intruder broke in, took the keys, copied them for future visits, and returned them to the wrong hook."

"Last night." Eden nudged Mallory. "You were checking doors and windows. You were looking for signs of a break-in, weren't you?"

"Wait—you—you knew I was outside? Was that *you* creeping around behind me?"

"I wasn't creeping around!" Eden paused. "Well, I guess I was. I couldn't sleep, and I was so restless I was afraid I'd wake Clint up, so I went to the living room. I was in my chair, reading on my phone. When I heard your door open, I turned the phone off. I didn't want to deal with you. I hoped you were just headed for the bathroom and wouldn't see me."

"You were in the living room?" Eden's favorite chair was in a corner next to the bookcase. Mallory couldn't remember paying any attention to the dark living room. "So I walked right past you?"

"Three times. When you slipped out the door the first time, I figured you were going to meet someone, and that was the last straw. We'd warned you. It was time to get the police involved. I was sitting there trying to decide whether to call them immediately or wait until morning or wake up Clint to discuss it with him—and then you came back inside."

"And got the stepstool," Mallory said.

"Yes, and now I was curious along with furious, and I decided to follow you."

Mallory disconnected her arm from Eden's and rubbed her temples. "You follow about as quietly as a herd of deer tromping through the woods."

"I didn't dare turn on my phone flashlight," Eden snapped. "It's hard to walk quietly when you can't see what you're stepping on. And I *did* watch you for a good few minutes before you got spooked, and *you're* the one who walked right past me three times without noticing a thing, so I don't think either one of us gets ninja points."

"Ninja points," Mallory repeated. She and Eden both started laughing.

"Let's keep it together, please," Clint said.

Eden took a packet of tissues out of her purse and wiped her eyes. "Then you locked me out. Thanks."

"Oops."

"I could've gotten inside by using the garage code, but I decided to wait on the porch for a while, to see if you would come out again. And to give myself a chance to calm down."

Mallory's brain generated a split-screen image of herself hunched on her bedroom floor and Eden hunched on the porch. By the time Eden had come inside, Mallory must have dozed off. "We're both ridiculous," Mallory said. "Maybe we could finish checking the windows together, in the daylight. Your yard is super eerie at 1:00 a.m."

"Tell me about it," Eden said.

"I didn't find any signs of forced entry on the doors and windows I did check. Wait a second—my bedroom window! Eden, last week, remember you found it open. I'd forgotten to shut it before I went to campus. Maybe if Lori—or someone—was casing the house, she saw the window open, got in the house that way, then took the key and made a copy."

Darien gripped Mallory's shoulder. "Could be."

Mallory looked up at him. "I need to check my bedroom. My desk is right underneath that window. There might be dirt smudges or other evidence on the desk or near it."

"Let's do that." Clint rose to his feet. "With the police present. I'm calling them now."

Mallory nodded.

CHAPTER 11

THE NEXT DAY, MALLORY STRUGGLED to stay awake in class. The interviews with the police and the officers' visit to the house had filled yesterday evening, and the clacks and clangs of an emergency locksmith had created distracting background noise as she'd attempted to do her homework. She'd finally fallen asleep at the kitchen table well past her usual bedtime. Dragging herself out of bed for her 4:00 a.m. shift had felt like trying to jump-start a zombie.

She had no idea what Eden, Clint, or Darien had said to Detective Jennifer Raley when she'd interviewed each of them, but the fact that Mallory wasn't trying to post bail right now had to be a positive sign. The police had found a shred of mulch behind Mallory's desk, which wasn't exactly proof, but it was enough to assure Mallory she'd been right about how the intruder had gotten into the house. The police had also dusted for fingerprints, but Mallory hadn't yet heard if any of the prints were Lori Sanders's. Mallory doubted it; Lori probably would have worn gloves. If the police couldn't find any clear evidence against Lori—or another culprit—blame would land right back on Mallory.

By the time she reached her Wednesday evening class, she couldn't concentrate at all. She could only watch the darkening sky through the classroom window, wonder foggily if Detective Raley had learned anything, and daydream about how comfortable it would feel to rest her face on the desk. For the first half of class, only sips of icy water from her water bottle kept her conscious.

For the second half of class, uneasiness about Eden canceled out drowsiness. Eden was home alone now, since Mallory's class didn't end until eight and Clint taught until nine. There was no reason to think Lori would dare show up when someone was obviously home. If she wanted face-to-face revenge, she'd have confronted Mallory, not schemed off-stage to get her in trouble. But growing worries troubled Mallory until she pulled her phone out and sent a text under the desk. Eden responded that she was fine and doing laundry. Mallory told her to double-check that the doors and windows were locked, to which Eden responded with an eye-roll emoji and an "I already did."

Mallory focused on her professor and tried again to listen. *Stop being paranoid,* she admonished herself. *If Lori's seen by anyone, she destroys her whole scheme. She won't come near the house while Eden is home.*

When Mallory reached her car after class, she found rain-wet leaves coating the windows. Anxious to get home, she rapidly cleared the leaves off by hand, not trusting her wimpy wiper blades. With her window opened a few inches so fresh, cool air would blow in her face, Mallory drove home and parked at the curb in her usual, not-where-Clint-liked-to-put-the-trash-bins spot.

For a moment, she studied the house. Light glowed from behind closed curtains. No strange cars were in sight. The porch light illuminated Eden's apple wreath—Mallory still needed to repair that chip—as well as the urns of yellow and rust-colored chrysanthemums and the damp red bricks of the steps. Everything looked normal. *What did you expect? Lori sitting in the porch rocking chair?*

Mallory stuffed her keys into the front pocket of her sweatshirt and reached to pick up her backpack.

The back, driver's-side door burst open, a blur of motion landed in the back seat of the car, and the door slammed. Mallory shrieked and grabbed for her door handle, but a hand caught her hair, jerking her backward and pinning her to the headrest. Something sharp and cold touched the side of her neck. It felt like the blade of a knife.

"Shut up." A male voice. "Don't move, or I'll cut your throat."

She froze. Who was he? Had she been wrong about Lori? No—Lori had left town with her boyfriend; this could be him.

"Do everything I say, and I won't hurt you. No noise. Got it?"

Mallory drew a gasping breath, smelling onions and beer. "Yes."

He released her hair and drew the knife away. "Hold out your right hand. Hold it next to your shoulder. Got something for you."

Mallory lifted her hand. Metal clacked and a heavy object dropped into her palm. She glanced at what he'd given her. Handcuffs.

"You're going to cuff yourself to the steering wheel," he said.

Panic tangled her thoughts. She fought to untangle them. "The police know about Lori, and they know about you," Mallory said, fishing for confirmation. "They know you left Gilroy together."

He swore under his breath. No questions, no denial. She'd been right.

"If you leave now, they won't catch you." Through the windshield, Mallory scanned the neighborhood, praying to see someone getting their mail or walking their dog.

"Cuff yourself to the steering wheel."

"Why?"

"Gotta make sure you stay put."

"Until what happens?"

With the tip of the knife, he poked her in the back of the neck. "Hurry."

Mallory reached as though to lock one link of the handcuffs around the steering wheel. She let her sweaty fingers bumble with the handcuffs, dropping them.

"You're stalling." He grabbed her by the hair and yanked her head back between the seats. "No more stalling. Got it?"

"Yes." She turned her head, trying to pull away, and glimpsed a capped syringe and a crumpled strip of rubber lying on the seat next to him.

He released her. "Pick up the handcuffs."

She bent forward and retrieved them. "Where's Lori?"

"Doing her part, babe. It's eye-for-an-eye time."

An eye for an eye? Slowly, Mallory clicked one link of the handcuffs shut around the steering wheel. Mallory had taken Lori's brother—and he was dead. Chills whirled through her, comprehension spinning into horror. *Eden.* Her fear for Eden had been on target. Lori was in there with Eden now. How had Lori gotten inside?

"Cuff your right wrist. Now."

Mallory switched hands so her left hand was maneuvering the handcuffs. That syringe in the backseat must be for her. Clint would find her next to Eden's body, too high or too woozy to leave the scene of the crime. It would look like Eden and Mallory had fought. Mallory would be blamed for Eden's death. *That* was what the planted drugs had been about: making Clint, and now the police, suspicious of Mallory. Lori's revenge was Eden's death *and* Mallory's conviction for murder.

Mallory had to get to Eden. Immediately.

The knife returned to its place against the side of her neck. Mallory adjusted the open link of the handcuffs as though to shut it around her wrist, then shot her right hand upward and backward as hard as she could, aiming for the man's face. Her knuckles slammed into bone. Pain burst in her hand and neck, but the knife twitched away from her. Mallory flung her door open. He caught the hood of her sweatshirt and yanked her back.

Screaming, Mallory swung her arm behind her, knocking the knife away. Pain blazed across the back of her hand. Twisting in her seat, she used her left hand to snatch the metal water bottle from the cup holder. The knife slashed through her right sleeve. Mallory smashed the bottle into his face. He reeled. She pounded twice more, and he collapsed against the seat, losing his grip on her sweatshirt.

Mallory lunged out of the car and sprinted toward the house. As she ran, she fumbled in her pocket for her keys, but when she reached the front door, she found it unlocked. She shoved the door open. "*Eden!*"

"Mallory!" Eden's cry came from the back of the house. "Call the police!"

Mallory couldn't; her phone was in her backpack in the car. "Get away from her, Lori!" Mallory yelled, grabbing the nearest weapon she could find—Eden's golf umbrella, from the stand near the front door. Mallory raced down the hall. "*Leave her alone!*"

A thud made the floor vibrate. Eden screamed. Another thud—from Eden's bedroom.

Mallory hurtled through the doorway as Lori yanked Eden to her knees and moved behind her. At the sight of a knife against Eden's throat, Mallory reeled, flapping the umbrella as she tried to halt her rush forward. She steadied herself a couple yards from Lori and Eden.

"Keep back," Lori said. "I'll kill her, Mallory."

Eden's face was gray, and she held her left arm stiff and still against her chest. The contents of her jewelry drawer glittered across the carpet, and her purse had been dumped on the bed. The nightstand lay on its side.

Panting for air, Mallory made a labored effort to speak calmly. "This problem is . . . ours . . . not Eden's. She never even met Nelson."

Lori met Mallory's gaze. Lori's eyes were like Nelson's, dark and beautiful and big. Memories sprung up inside Mallory: the countless times she'd teased Nelson about his Disney-character eyes.

"An umbrella?" Lori's low, flinty voice sounded strange to Mallory. She realized she'd expected to hear the childishly innocent voice that had been part of Lori's get-out-of-trouble toolbox. "Wow, scary. Couldn't you find something deadlier, like a pool noodle? Drop it."

Mallory dropped the umbrella, not pointing out that if it were harmless, Lori wouldn't care if Mallory held it.

"Where is Jasper?" Lori asked.

"Jas—your guy friend? Bleeding in my car, probably."

"Mal," Eden croaked, "you're hurt."

Mallory glanced at the blood trickling off her hand and felt like apologizing for the damage she was doing to the carpet. "I'm okay."

"Your neck."

She touched the bleeding cut on the side of her neck. "It's shallow. I'm okay." *I hope it's shallow.* She edged closer to Eden and Lori. "The police are on their way," she bluffed. "Let Eden go. Do you want a murder charge?"

"Did Nels want a murder charge? You gave him one."

"Then let Eden go and deal with me."

"This *is* dealing with you, you dumb maggot."

Mallory eyed the knife at Eden's throat. It was one of Eden's well-sharpened knives from the knife block on the kitchen counter. "Your frame-up scheme has already failed. I won't go to prison no matter what you do. Kill her and *you'll* go to prison for life, while I live a long life of freedom."

A panicky ripple jarred Lori's voice. "I'll—I'll kill you both."

"No. You won't. If you hurt my sister, you'll be lucky if the police get here in time to stop *me* from hurting *you.*"

Lori snorted. "What will you do? Poke me with your umbrella?"

"This is your one shot at me. Take it." Mallory hoped she didn't look as shaky and sick as she felt. "Or be smart and run before the cops get here."

Outside, a man shouted from the direction of the street, his words muffled by window glass. Another shout—two voices.

Lori cursed. She grabbed Eden by the collar of her blouse and heaved her to the side. Eden shrieked, her injured arm twitching as she tried to catch herself. Her head struck the side of the overturned nightstand.

Lori leaped toward Mallory. Mallory snatched the umbrella off the floor and swung it. It struck Lori's forearm, diverting the arc of the knife. Lori swung the knife a second time. Mallory blocked it; the blade sliced through waterproofed nylon and pinged against the umbrella's metal ribs.

Lori seized the end of the umbrella with her empty hand and tried to wrench it out of Mallory's grasp, but Lori couldn't overpower Mallory's two-handed grip. Lori dropped the knife, clamped both hands around the umbrella and ripped it out of Mallory's hold. Mallory dove for the knife. Lori kicked the knife across the room and hammered the umbrella across Mallory's shoulders, pounding her to the floor.

Mallory glimpsed Eden springing toward Lori. Lori crashed the umbrella into Eden's arm. Agony in her scream, Eden stumbled sideways. Mallory launched herself at Lori and flattened her face-down onto the carpet.

"Eden, grab the knife!" Mallory yelled as she pinned Lori beneath her and struggled to rip the umbrella out of Lori's hands. "Her boyfriend might be in here any second—Call the police, I didn't have time—"

Lori swept the umbrella to the side, eluding Mallory's hands, and attempted to swing it backward to strike her. Mallory grabbed again for it, but her injured hand was growing clumsy.

Eden seized the knife and lurched toward the fight. With the knife in her fist, she dropped to her knees next to Lori's head. "Let . . . go of . . . the . . . umbrella." Gasps of pain pushed Eden's words apart. "Quit fighting . . . or I'll pay you . . . back for . . . breaking my arm."

Lori released the umbrella, but her body remained tense, ready to resist. Mallory captured one of her wrists and wrenched her arm up behind her back.

The front door banged against the doorstop, and an agitated voice shouted, "Mallory! Eden!"

Darien?

"Back here!" Mallory yelled. Footsteps thundered down the hall. "Watch out! There's a guy with a knife—"

"Under control." Darien raced through the door of the bedroom, a knife in *his* hand. Seeing Mallory on top of Lori, he moved toward them. "You're bleeding—"

"I'm okay. I'm not bleeding to death. Grab something to tie her up."

"Use my purse strap." Eden tilted her head toward the bed.

Mallory spotted a purplish bruise swelling near Eden's hairline. "You hit your head. Are you—"

"It just stunned me for a moment. My arm is what's injured. I'm sorry, Mal. The bell rang, there was a package on the porch . . . I thought it was just a delivery and opened the door. She was there, out of sight . . . I'm such a fool."

Darien took Eden's empty purse off the bed and unclipped the long shoulder strap. "I'll hold her hands. Mallory, can you tie them?"

"I think so." The stinging pain of her injuries seemed to be escalating, and her fingers shook as she took the purse strap.

"The police are on their way," Darien added.

Lori muttered a string of profanity, but to Mallory's surprise, the words were aimed not at her but at Jasper. Darien gripped Lori's wrists and pressed them together. Mallory wound the purse strap around them. Gritting her teeth, she tugged the strap tight.

"Here, I'll do the rest." Darien took the ends of the strap and knotted them.

Lori rested her cheek against the carpet, and the tautness in her body finally slackened. Was Mallory's eyesight going rogue, or was that relief in Lori's face?

"Nelson thought the world revolved around you." In Lori's now-gravelly tone, Mallory heard grief, not rage. "Do you think he *meant* to hurt your mom? Do you think he deserved what he got?"

"No," Mallory said. "I never thought that."

Heavy footsteps thumped from the front of the house, accompanied by a shout. "Police!"

Mallory crawled off Lori and collapsed into Darien's arms.

CHAPTER 12

SWATHED IN A FLEECE BLANKET, Mallory leaned against Darien and sleepily watched the flames in Eden's fireplace. Most of her body ached, but as long as she didn't move, the soreness didn't pierce through her fatigue. She kept falling asleep and waking up, drawn repeatedly back to consciousness by her determination to wait for Clint and Eden to return from the hospital.

Darien kept both arms around her, his fingers interlocked. "You should go to bed," he said. "I brought you home to get some rest."

"I want to make sure Eden's all right."

"She'll be fine. All the news has been good."

"So far." At the time Mallory and Darien had left the ER, Eden hadn't been showing any signs of a concussion and the doctor had determined that the break in her arm would heal without surgery.

"You know Clint will call if anything changes," Darien said.

"I know. But I need to see her."

"I understand. Mallory, I'm sorry I was too slow to keep you and Eden from getting hurt—"

"Quit it." He'd been blaming himself all evening. "You were the one perceptive enough to realize we were in danger, that it wasn't likely that Lori would go to that much trouble and then be satisfied with getting me arrested for possession."

"If I'd been perceptive a little earlier, instead of waiting until your class ended to drive over here—"

"Shh. You tackled that creep boyfriend. If he'd gotten inside, Eden and I would have been in a lot more trouble."

"I didn't do much. He was so dizzy from your beating, he could barely walk. How was Lori so accurate in timing her attack? She must have known when you had class and that you'd be home before Clint."

"The calendar on the fridge, I think. Eden writes everything there. Lori must have seen it when she broke in earlier to leave the drugs. She took the spare keys off the board on the side of the fridge, so she definitely would have seen the calendar."

"And committed the criminal blunder of forgetting to note the difference between the 'house keys' hook and the 'spare house keys' hook. Many crimes fail when criminals underestimate their target's organizational skills."

Mallory smiled. "Well, it wasn't a critical error, but it did go a long way toward getting Clint and Eden to consider my innocence. And Lori gets credit for improvising after she found out we'd changed the locks."

"Stealing a package off a neighbor's porch, planting it here, ringing the bell, hiding," Darien said. "Not bad."

"Poor Eden. I told her to stop feeling guilty. I would have opened the door too. We order so much online that there's always something getting delivered, and we had no idea Lori would confront anyone face-to-face. We were worried about her breaking in, not ringing the doorbell." A feeble resurgence of adrenaline spread through Mallory. She gave it a moment to ebb so she could speak cheerfully. "Darien, I'm usually a pretty normal person. After the past few days, you must think I'm a disaster."

He chuckled. "Am I giving you that impression right now?"

"No, but you're a nice guy, good at comforting a friend."

His arms loosened, and he turned to look at her. Firelight revealed apprehension in his face, but his voice was even. "Is friendship all you want from me? Whatever the facts are, I can deal with them, but please tell me the truth."

"Darien, I wore makeup at *four in the morning* for you."

"You did?"

"You didn't even notice it, did you? Or the cute clothes? I give up. I'm just rolling out of bed and going to work in my pajamas from now on."

He laughed. "You always look beautiful. Even wearing—" He checked the clothing sticking out from the blanket. "Sweat pants and . . . bandages and . . . I don't know what shirt you're wearing."

"A Disneyland T-shirt that used to belong to my cousin." Mallory leaned toward Darien, and their lips touched.

His kiss was tender. Mallory reached to put her arms around him, but the motion made the stitches in her hand and arm burn and aggravated her bruises.

At the unsteadiness in her movements, Darien drew back. "I'm sorry. You're hurting, and you're a little out of it from stress and sleep deprivation. Anything more than a handshake tonight is less than gentlemanly."

"I have six stitches in my hand, and my knuckles are bruised," she said. "I don't want a handshake."

He kissed her cheek. "Rest." He pulled the blanket back around her and drew her into his arms.

She rested her head against his shoulder and closed her eyes.

About the Author

STEPHANIE BLACK HAS LOVED BOOKS since she was old enough to grab the pages, and has enjoyed creating make-believe adventures since she and her sisters were inventing long Barbie games filled with intrigue and danger or running around pretending to be detectives. She is a four-time Whitney Award winner for Best Mystery/Suspense and a finalist for Best Speculative Fiction.

Stephanie was born in Utah and has lived in various places, including Arkansas, Arizona, Massachusetts, and Limerick, Ireland. She currently lives in northern California. She plays the violin in a community symphony, enjoys dark chocolate, and loves spending time with her husband, Brian, and their family, currently consisting of five kids, three kids-in-law, a cat, and three grandpets.

Stephanie enjoys hearing from her readers. You can contact her via email at info@covenant-lds.com or by mail care of Covenant Communications, P.O. Box 416, American Fork, UT 84003-0416.

stephanieblack.net
facebook.com/stephanieblackauthor